THIS CANDLEWICK BOOK BELONGS TO:

_____

_____

_____

_____

For Charlotte and her best friend, Kelly

First U.S. paperback edition 1994

Published in Great Britain in 1992 by Walker Books Ltd., London.

The Library of Congress has cataloged the hardcover edition as follows:

Graham, Bob.
Rose meets Mr. Wintergarten / by Bob Graham — 1st U.S. ed.
Summary: A young girl's attempt to retrieve her ball from
her grouchy, old neighbor's yard changes the way they feel about each other.
ISBN 1-56402-039-8 (hardcover). — ISBN 1-56402-395-8 (paperback)
[1. Neighborliness — Fiction. 2. Old age — Fiction.] I. Title.
PZ7.G751667Ro   1992
[E]—dc20   91-71824

2 4 6 8 10 9 7 5 3

Printed in Hong Kong

This book was typeset in Plantin.
The illustrations were done in watercolor and pen.

Candlewick Press
2067 Massachusetts Avenue
Cambridge, Massachusetts 02140

Rose

Meets Mr. Wintergarten

by Bob Graham

CANDLEWICK PRESS
CAMBRIDGE, MASSACHUSETTS

The morning the Summers family moved into their new house, they felt at home. Faith and Rose put up their pictures. Baby Blossom watched.

Mr. and Mrs. Summers planted pansies, petunias, daisies, and geraniums. Their garden was a carpet of flowers. All before the sun went down.

Every morning from the roof of their house, the
Summerses watched the sun come up.

The sun never touched the house next door. Next door everything bristled. Next door lived Mr. Wintergarten.

There were stories in the street about Mr. Wintergarten.

"He's mean,"
said Emily.

"And horrible,"
said Arthur.

"He's got a dog like a wolf," said Naomi.

"And a saltwater crocodile."

"They say he rides on his crocodile at night," said Emily.
"And GETS YA!" Arthur shrieked.
"I don't believe you," said Rose. "Anyway, don't frighten Blossom."

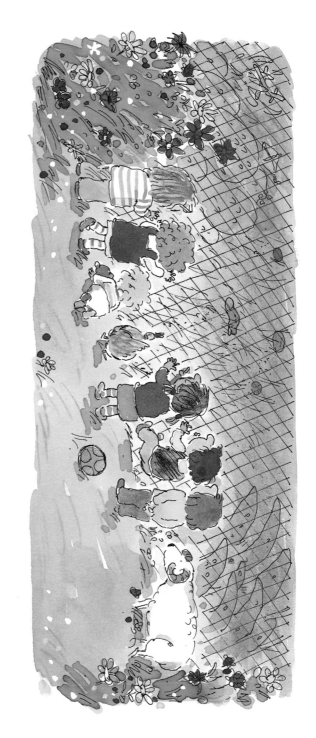

"My dad lost his football over there when he was a boy," said Emily. "You can just see it through the prickles, old and flat as a pancake."

"No one ever goes in there," said Arthur, "in case Mr. Wintergarten eats people."

"If your ball ever goes over," said Naomi, "forget it."

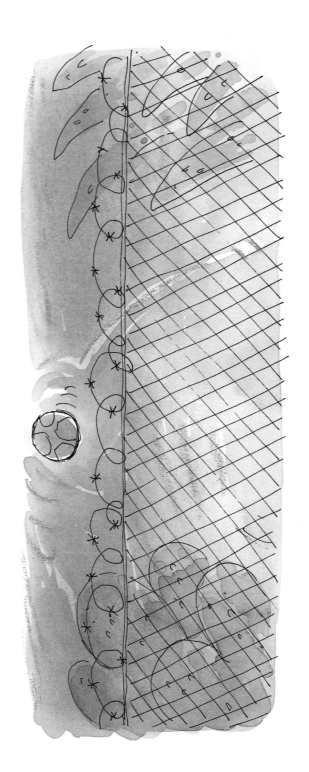

And just then, Rose's ball went straight over
Mr. Wintergarten's fence!

Rose went to tell her mom.

"Well, honeybunch," Mom said, "you can get your ball back. Why don't you just go and *ask* him?"

"Because he eats kids," said Rose.

"We'll take him some cookies instead," said Mom.

"And maybe some flowers."

Mr. Wintergarten's front gate had not been opened for years. Rose heaved and pushed. The gate groaned and squeaked. Then slowly it swung open.

Rose could see that there *was* a dog – big as a wolf!

"I don't see any crocodile," she said.

"I should hope not," replied Mom, and threw the dog a cookie.

Rose knocked at Mr. Wintergarten's door.

"Who the devil is that?" shouted a voice from inside.

"It's me," said Rose, and tiptoed in.

"What do *you* want?" said Mr. Wintergarten.
"I'm Rose Summers from next door. I've come to
ask for my ball back."

She twisted her fingers in her handkerchief.
"I've brought some flowers, and cookies from
my mom."
Mr. Wintergarten glared at her.

His dinner was cold, gray, and uninviting, with gristle floating in it and mosquitoes breeding on top. But Rose could see that he wasn't eating children.

"Please may I look for my ball?" she asked.
"No," growled Mr. Wintergarten. "Go away!"

But when Rose had gone, Mr. Wintergarten slowly
pushed back his chair – and did something he
hadn't done in years …

Mr. Wintergarten opened his curtains.

He saw Rose's ball
and thoughtfully pushed
it with his toe.

Next he made some darting
movements that made his
coattails fly in the sun.

He sat on his front step in the sun. "No one has
ever asked for their ball back," he said to himself.
"Or brought cookies."

And then, Mr. Wintergarten kicked the ball ...

right back over the fence!

"Great kick!" said Rose.
"Nice catch!" said Mr. Wintergarten.

"Would you mind throwing back my slipper?" he added.

"Catch, Mr. Wintergarten!" said Rose,
throwing back the slipper.

"Good throw, Rose!" said Mr. Wintergarten.
"Let's play again tomorrow."

Gr

Graham, Bob.
Rose meets Mr.
Wintergarten.

DATE

BAKER & TAYLOR